The Ballet Recital

By Jenne Simon
Illustrated by Prescott Hill

SCHOLASTIC INC.

New York   Toronto   London   Auckland

Sydney   Mexico City   New Delhi   Hong Kong

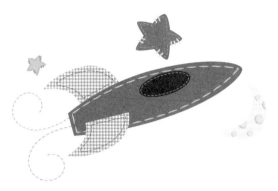

ISBN 978-0-545-39216-7

12 11 10 9 8 7 6 5 4 3 2 1   12 13 14 15 16 17/0

Designed by Angela Jun
Printed in the U.S.A.   40
First printing, January 2012

It was a great day in Lalaloopsy Land.
Tippy Tumblelina's friends had come
over to play!
"What should we do?" asked Dot Starlight.

Jewel Sparkles wanted to play dress up.
Spot Splatter Splash wanted to draw.
Pillow Featherbed wanted to take a nap.
But Tippy could not sit still.

Tippy's toes were tapping.
She twirled and jumped and kicked.
"I wish I could dance like that," said Dot.

"I have a great idea!" said Tippy.
"I'll teach you some steps. Then we can put on a show outside for our friends."

"How perfectly perfect!" said Jewel.
"I can't wait!" said Spot.
"Zzzzzz!" said Pillow.

"Let's start with some easy steps," said Tippy.
She showed them how to stretch.
Then she showed them how to point.

"Now let's try some harder steps," said Tippy.
She showed them how to spin.
Then she showed them how to leap.

"Dancing is fun," said Spot.

"It's magical," said Jewel.

"It is almost time to put on the show!" said Tippy.

But Dot had her head in the clouds.
And Pillow kept falling asleep.
"I don't know all the steps yet," said Dot.
"Me neither," said Pillow.

"Don't worry," said Tippy. "I'll help you both."
"Great," said Pillow. "But first I need a nap."

Jewel and Spot tiptoed out the door.
They were going to invite their friends to see the show.

Pillow woke up from her nap.

"I had the best dream," she said. "I knew all the steps!"

"Let's make that dream come true," said Tippy.

Tippy showed her the steps again.

Stretch! Point! Spin! Leap!

"Am I dreaming?" asked Pillow. "I think I've got it!"

Then Tippy went over the steps with Dot.
Stretch! Point! Spin! Leap!
Dot tried to follow Tippy's lead.

Stretch! Point! Spin! CRASH!
"I am just not getting the steps," cried Dot.
"I'm afraid I'll ruin the show!"

"No, you won't," said Tippy. "Want to know why?"
Dot nodded.
"You are just like me," said Tippy. "You love to fly."
"That's true," said Dot.

Tippy went on. "When you leap, pretend you are on a rocket ship soaring through space."

Dot smiled. "Tippy, you are full of great ideas!"

Jewel and Spot were back!
And they had lots of friends with them.

Crumbs Sugar Cookie, Peanut Big Top, Bea Spells-a-Lot, and Mittens Fluff 'n' Stuff could not wait to see the show.

Crumbs even made some sweet treats for all the dancers.

Then the lights dimmed and everyone found a seat.
The show was about to begin!

Dot peeked around the curtain.
All her friends were there.
"I'm scared," she said. "What if I forget the steps?"

"I get scared, too," said Tippy.
"And sometimes I make mistakes.
But I always try my best and have lots of fun."

Tippy smiled at Dot.
"That's what makes a girl a star!"

"It's showtime, girls!" said Tippy.
The dancers took their places.
The music began to play.

One by one, the girls began to dance. Pillow stretched. Spot pointed. Jewel spun. Tippy leaped.

Now it was Dot's turn.
She closed her eyes.
She was on a rocket ship.

And she was flying through space!

Everyone cheered!
"Looks like our show was a hit," said Tippy.

"Thanks to you," said Dot.
"I tried my best and I had a lot of fun!"

"You flew!" said Tippy. "And you know what that means?"

"What?" asked Dot.

Tippy smiled. "You are a star!"